DEDICATION

To my dear family and one hundred closest friends.
May the kindness and love you have shown me
come back to you one hundred fold!

With Much Love,

Annie

"Hang On If You Want To Come Along!"

Written by Annie Jacobsen
Illustrated by Kathryn "Kat" Londo

The Author and Publisher wish to thank
Dennis Schmidt for his graphic design and computer savvy, and
Jon Knutson, Mary Buchholz, Norma Sampson and Sandra Oemichen for their editing and proof-reading skills.
A heartfelt thanks also to Frederick and Joanna Rouse and Kathie Gallagher for their encouragement, help, support,
and forbearance these past years during my weekend absences and adventures in marketing.
Kat, thank you for all your hard work on this project.
The Pickled Herring Press Logo and name are trademarks
of Annie Jacobsen and Susan Jo Hanson
Contact: Ann Rouse
annies49@yahoo.com
www.pickledherringpress.com
Fitchburg, Wisconsin

Library of Congress Control Number: 2008920426
ISBN-13: 978-0-9778276-2-6
Publisher's Cataloging-In-Publication Data
(Prepared by The Donohue Group, Inc.)
Jacobsen, Annie T.
Hang on if you want to come along! / written by Annie Jacobsen ; illustrated by Kat Londo.
p. : col. ill. ; cm.

Summary: The Princess Nell has not laughed or even smiled for many years but, at last, King Gunnar and young Erik have a plan to change all that.
ISBN: 978-0-9778276-2-6
1. Princesses--Juvenile fiction. 2. Laughter--Juvenile fiction. 3. Princesses--Fiction. 4. Laughter--Fiction. I. Londo, Kat. II. Title.

PZ7.J33 Ha 2008
PS3610.A26 H36 2008
[E] 2008920426

Printed in Hong Kong

Hang On If You Want To Come Along!

Written by Annie Jacobsen
Illustrated by Kathryn "Kat" Londo

Pickled Herring Press
Madison, Wisconsin

In Oven, near Oslo, I've heard tell,
There lived a great King and his daughter Nell.
The Princess was lovely, gracious and fine,
But she never smiled. She was sad all the time.

Nell would sit at her window each day and sigh.
She never would smile or laugh or cry.
Her father, King Gunnar, was filled with concern.
He longed to hear her laughter return.

The King had tried everything at his command,
From jokesters to jesters doing handstands,
To make Nell crack just one little smile,
And give into laughter just for a while.

Royal Contest
Win half
of a kingdom!
plus...

Finally, at wit's end, he created a stir
By holding a contest to amuse her.
The lad who could make his daughter laugh
Would win her hand and his kingdom by half.

The word went out through out the land,
And would be suitors were soon on hand.
Though many tried to bring a smile to her face,
They all went home, heads hung in disgrace.

Now outside of Oven there lived a man,
Just a poor farmer, who worked the land.
He had three sons, two were wise and one not,
They were all quite lazy and left the fields to rot.

Esben, the eldest, just played his fiddle all day.
When his father asked for help, he would just say,
"Oh Father, dear Father please do not fret,
I will marry the Princess and we will be set."

"I will play for Nell happy little tunes,
Then she will laugh until she swoons.
The king shall reward me with her hand
And half the kingdom, that's a lot of land!"

So off Esben went to play for the Princess,
To make her smile and lose her senses.
And play he did 'til his fingers ached,
Alas, no smile was his, only heartbreak.

Back home he went with his head hung low.
Back to the fields to make the crops grow.
No more big dreams to marry Princess Nell,
But he still played his music and did it quite well.

The second son, Arne, was an artist by trade.
He made people look silly in the drawings he made.
He'd sell them at market for extra spending money.
They made people laugh. They thought they were funny.

Arne had been practicing for quite a while.
He knew his drawings would make the Princess smile,
Then they would be wed and have half the kingdom.
He'd have money to spare and a bride that was winsome.

So off Arne went to draw for the Princess,
To make her smile and lose her senses.
And draw he did 'til his fingers ached,
Alas, no smile was his, only heartbreak.

Back home he went with his head hung low.
Back to the fields to make the crops grow.
No more big dreams to marry the Princess Nell,
But he drew what pleased him, and did it quite well.

The youngest son, Erik, had been carefully watching.
He'd seen his brothers fail and a plan he was hatching.
Though Erik could neither draw nor music play,
He went about things in an unusual way.

Off to the castle young Erik went to work,
He was given a job with the cook and the clerk.
One day the cook sent him to catch a fine fish,
One that she'd cook for the King's supper dish.

Erik went down to a nearby stream,
And spotted a fish, big as a dream.
He carefully caught it in his net,
Then started back with the biggest fish yet!

Along the way he met an old woman with her pet.
It was the handsomest Elkhound he'd ever met.
She suggested a trade, the dog for his fish,
Erik quickly agreed, so they made the switch.

Before she left Erik, she told him a tale.
The dog was magic! She'd bought him at a sale.
When anyone wanted to pet the dog, Erik must say,
"Hang on if you want to come along. Let's be on our way!"

The person would then be stuck fast to the dog,
And, no matter what, they'd have to follow along.
The spell would be broken only by Nell's laughter,
Then the two of them would live happily ever after.

Erik thanked the old woman as she turned away,
Then he took up the leash and started on his way.
Past farms and fields Erik and his Elkhound went,
On towards the village and past the Lake Kent.

As soon as they approached Oven town,
Out stepped the Butcher with an "eye of round."
"What a fine Elkhound you have there, Erik!
May I please pet him, just for a minute?"

And as the Butcher reached down to pet the dog,
Erik's voice rang out loud and strong,
"Hang on if you want to come along. Let's be on our way!"
The Butcher was stuck fast, he had no say.

Along the cobbled street they went,
Until the town's Baker next they met.
"What happened to the Butcher, Erik dear?
He's not happy, that is more than clear."

Erik said, "He appears to be stuck quite fast.
Can you free him? It's a difficult task."
The Baker grabbed the Butcher by the waist.
She pulled 'til she was red in the face.

Erik just smiled and then he said,
The words that would glue her to the dog's head.
"Hang on if you want to come along, Let's be on our way!"
Now the Baker was stuck fast, she had no say.

Erik and his fine Elkhound, who was quite tame,
Continued along looking just the same.
But the Butcher now was hopping along,
With the Baker attached to him good and strong.

Just as they passed the Barber shop,
The Barber ran out and hollered,"Stop!"
"What's this madness that's possessed you all?
You all look like fools about to fall!"

"Let me help you before you spill your rolls!"
So he grabbed the Baker and tugged and pulled.
Erik said,"Hang on if you want to come along! Let's be on our way,"
So the Barber was stuck fast, he had no say.

Down the road they all came,
Erik led the Elkhound, who looked the same.
The Butcher, Baker and the Barber all three,
Looking like fools for all to see.

The townspeople gathered and followed the troop,
Pointing and laughing at the strange looking group.
Erik and his Elkhound led the parade,
Can't you imagine the strange sight they made?

On to the castle the group did march,
Across the moat and under the arch.
On into the courtyard where the Princess sat,
Looking sad and alone in her pretty blue hat.

The arrogant Butler was just serving tea,
As the group approached he said,"Oh dear me!
I suppose I must try to free these poor fools,"
So he grabbed the Barber as he passed Nell's stool.

T' was then Erik shouted,"Hang on if you want to come along. Let's be on our way!"
So the proper Butler was stuck fast. He had no say.
With his head held high and a stiff upper lip,
He followed the others trying hard not to trip.

As the Princess sat watching all this commotion,
A small smile appeared as she watched the procession.
She called for her father to come quickly and see,
This mismatched group, marching 'round her tree.

Her father, King Gunnar, came running right out
To see what all the great noise was all about.
Then Nell did something she hadn't done in years,
She laughed right out loud 'til her eyes ran with tears.

As the King and the crowd looked on in amazement,
The spell was broken and the group hit the pavement.
The Butcher let go of the dog at last,
And the Baker let go of the Butcher fast!

The Barber let go of the Baker, too
And the Butler, not knowing what else to do,
Served the whole crowd crumpets and tea,
While the Princess sat chuckling happy and free.

The King called to Erik,"Come here my lad!
You've won my fair Nell by making her glad.
Half the kingdom is yours, just as I said,
A week from today, the Princess you'll wed."

"Thank you, your Highness, that would be swell!
I promise to love and cherish dear Nell.
My father and brothers will be happy to hear,
That I've completed this task and they can live here!"

The very next week the wedding was held.
They lived happily ever after. There's no more to tell!

Peter Christen Asbjornsen and Jorgen Moe have created a world famous collection of traditional Norwegian Folktales. The Tales are often gruesome, and disturbingly violent, as are those original tales of the Brother's Grimm. None-the-less, they remain classics in Norwegian Folklore. They were first translated over one hundred years ago.

Their collection, "Norwegian Folk Tales 1 & 2" is available through Dreyers Forlag A/S, Fred. Olsensgt. 5, Postboks 1153 Sentrum, 0153 Oslo, Norway.
The additions I have were printed in 1990.
The ISBN# for #1 is 82-09-10598-1 and for #2 is 82-09-10600-7
Using the ISBN numbers, they can be ordered through any bookstore here in the States as well.

The illustrations were done by Theodor Kittelsen and Erik Werenskiold two of Norway's most accomplished artists. Most are pen and ink drawings that have a charming simplicity and yet they are detailed enough to stir the reader's imagination. They are beautifully executed.
These volumes should definitely be in every Norwegian Folk Tale Fan's library!